The price of insanity

By Z. Martin

The following story "Tap." Has been previously featured in "Stroll down the crooked path."

I caution you reader. There are events in these stories that some may find disturbing. Read at your own risk.

Table of contents

Introduction

Welcome to the twisted mind of Z. Martin. First, I would like to thank my wife for her constant support in my work. I would also like to thank everyone that read this before it came out, and gave me so many helpful tips. Lastly, I leave this reminder for my children, follow your dreams and never give up. I hope you enjoy these thirteen short stories. Are you ready to pay the price of insanity?

Getaway

A peaceful getaway in the woods was exactly what the doctor ordered. I'd had it all planned out. Some good friends, good booze, and some even better drugs. Oh, and snacks. Really, really good snacks. The doctor may have an issue with that drug part, but who hasn't lied to their doctor?

Ryan, Patrick, and I had tried just about every illegal substance we could get our hands on. College was supposed to be a time to find yourself and I'd decided to find myself through drugs. Ryan and Patrick happened to agree with my outlook on life and would chip in when needed.

Finals were over with, and we were all headed back to our hometowns one degree richer. I had the brilliant idea that before finals were over, we should all blow off steam together in one last hurrah. I wanted one final getaway with my friends before the real world took over.

So, there we stood, outside the cheapest cabin we could afford. Snacks packed, drinks overflowing, and some of the hardest psychedelics our dealer could find.

"This place is gross man," Ryan said wiping a spider web off his shirt sleeve. "You couldn't have found something a little nicer?"

"We are going to be stoned out of our minds most of the time. What does it matter if it's not the cleanest thing ever?" I mumbled as I struggled with the lock. After a few hard jiggles, the door came loose, and a wave of stale air rushed past us.

"I'll feel better once I get a few shots in me so hurry up," Patrick grumbled as he shoved past me. "We've been stuck in that musty piece of shit you call a car for the last two hours. This place smells like heaven compared to that."

Patrick placed the box of liquor on the table, glass clanking loudly, and grabbed the closest bottle. Ryan quickly located the cups while I began unpacking. Once I had the sleeping bags in and set aside, I joined the guys for some shots. Ryan and Patrick had already taken more than a few without me.

"Slow down guys, we have the whole weekend ahead of us," I pleaded observing the whiskey bottle already dangerously close to half empty.

"Chill, Matt," Patrick said as he threw back another shot. "Like you said we are going to be stoned half the time anyways," He eyed the pocket of my bag containing the pills. He set his glass down and sighed.

"Let's hope that guy knew what he was talking about."

I took the hint and pulled out the baggie. Tiny, blue unmarked tablets filled a very small corner of the baggie. I silently wondered if the dealer had been telling the truth, too, considering how much money I had handed over. He had assured me these little blue wonders would show me things I'd never seen before.

"Well, come on let's get this party started man," Patrick said as he eagerly swiped the baggie from my hands and dug in. He dropped the pill in his mouth, poured a shot of whiskey and swallowed.

Ryan joined him as I got myself a cup from the cabinet. I hesitated for a second to take in the scene. This would probably be the last time my friends and I would have a chance to do this. I wanted to savor every moment of it.

Ryan and Patrick stood around the table pouring each other shots. They laughed after each shot seeing the sour face the other had made. I grabbed the bottle and threw back several shots worth of cheap whiskey to catch up to them. I poured myself a cup and opened a bag of chips. The chip in my hand fell to the floor as a loud bang echoed outside the cabin. I rushed outside to check on the damage.

A small tree had randomly fallen over just behind the car. My old beat-up SUV wouldn't be bothered by a small dent here or there. I would have to remember to clear it out before we left though just in case it messed up the tires. I made my way back inside to check on the guys.

Ryan and Patrick were in a heated debate over which field of study would make the most profit. I took a seat in an old wooden chair across from them. The chair groaned under my weight like everything else here, the age of the cabin was taking its toll. I joined in with their debate adding my career choice into the mix.

After thirty minutes and several more drinks, we all began laughing at every little thing. The drugs and whiskey were taking over. This was going to be the most amazing getaway any of us had ever experienced.

"Time to break the seal guys." I groaned, sitting up and making my wall down the hall.

"What did the seals ever do to you man?" Patrick yelled after me.

I excused myself to the bathroom while the guys cracked up laughing about their idiotic joke.

I finished my business and looked into the mirror. Its grimy surface poorly reflected my patchy beard. As I stared harder into it, observing a rather large pimple, something caught my eye. As I got even closer to the mirror to try and make out what was in the reflection. I saw what looked like a bony red hand pulling back the shower curtain.

I spun around quickly and yanked the shower curtain back. I hadn't prepared myself and went stumbling as I did so. Whatever was in there would have taken me for supper if there had been anything in there. I stared at the empty tub trying to find anything that could have resembled the hand I'd just seen.

I pinched myself and forced myself to take deep, slow breaths. I was not going to let this turn into a bad trip. If I let anxiety and fear take over, I'd be fighting them the entire weekend while coming down from the pills. Out of the corner of my eye I saw a shadow dart down the hallway towards the living room. I tip toed towards the door trying not to make too much noise. A loud crunch of what I could only imagine to be bones echoed from underneath my feet.

The bag of chips I had dropped on the way to the bathroom stuck out from underneath my shoe. I turned the corner to the living room where Patrick and Ryan still sat laughing. Out of the corner of my eye, I saw a dark figure with a misshapen head dart back into the kitchen. I froze for a moment telling myself it was just my imagination; I was just having a bad trip and I needed to calm down.

"Yo Mat, have you met our friend Mr. Snacks yet?" Ryan roared with laughter.

"Mr. Snacks?" I repeated, blinking at him.

"Yeah man, he's this really skinny guy that keeps asking for snacks." Patrick said through a mouthful of chips "I keep telling him to grab a bag from the kitchen, but he doesn't listen too good."

Patrick and Ryan burst out laughing. I smiled, shook my head, and sat down with them. I snatched up the stray bottle that had been forgotten. I downed a generous helping and let the burn sink to my stomach.

"Have you guys been seeing anything creepy?" I asked them to ease my way in to talk about what I'd just seen in the bathroom.

"Not any creepier than Mr. Snacks over there." Patrick pointed towards the kitchen. "His face is all screwed up, but he's an okay guy."

"These pills are amazing Mat," Ryan said as he observed his hand. "You should go take yours."

I stared at Ryan for a moment. I'd taken my pill with them. I had stood there with them at the table after I'd pulled out the baggie and we'd knocked back the whiskey. I remember holding the pill in my hand and pouring myself the glass. I walked into the kitchen searching the room for the one they called Mr. Snacks. As I passed by the table, I noticed the empty bag. Well, the nearly empty bag. In the very corner of the bag sat a tiny blue pill.

I hadn't taken it. I had walked outside to figure out what the bang was earlier. I wasn't having a bad trip at all. So, if I wasn't having a bad trip what the hell was I seeing?

"Snacks."

The scratchy tone came from the living room, and I bolted toward the noise. Thinking Ryan and Patrick were messing around, I walked back to the living room to call them out. But Ryan was sitting in a daze seemingly unbothered as a misshapen man with red skin and stringy black hair nibbled on his index finger.

The man's teeth had been filed down to razor-sharp points. Fresh blood flowed in rivulets down Ryan's finger from the cuts the teeth were making. As I stared at the man, I noticed his skin wasn't red but was coated with dried red streaks.

The smell of week-old roadkill wafted from his direction.
The hunched man stopped for a moment and in a flash a
snap echoed throughout the cabin. Ryan's finger was no
longer attached. Patrick sat nearby holding out a chip bag
for the man as if he was trying to coax a dog.

The whiskey in my stomach turned to ice as fear took over
my entire body. I did the only thing I could think of to do-
run. I barely turned the knob before I forcefully shouldered
the door open and fell out onto the porch. Boards creaked
as I picked myself back up in a stumbling run to the SUV.

"Matt where are you going man? The party's just getting
started. Mr. snacks says he has some more friends that want
to come party with us!" I heard Patrick yelling after me. I
didn't bother with a response. He wouldn't have heard me
anyway.

As soon as I opened the car door, a panicked scream
echoed out from the cabin. I didn't wait to see if my friends
were coming. I knew from that scream that they had
learned what kind of snack Mr. Snacks had been looking
for. I threw the vehicle into reverse, but came to an abrupt
halt, wheels spinning.

I'd forgotten about the damn tree! I threw the SUV back
into drive and lurched forward. I looked back at the cabin
and saw the man standing on the porch. His red skin was
now slick from my friends' blood. He stood there hunched
over ribs prominently displayed. Razor sharp rows of teeth
on display for the world to see.

In one hand, he held Ryan's head- his goofy grin still displayed on it. In the other, he waved a severed hand in an imitation of goodbye. I saw him mouth the word "snacks," again. Light shone in his eyes as if he had a sudden stroke of genius. He lifted the severed hand to Ryan's lip and used the fingers to move the lips in a mockery of goodbye. Mr. Snacks howled laughter at his own joke. At the sound of his howl the trees and bushes surrounding the cabin began to shake and part.

I had enough time to see other red, hunched creatures start to emerge before I threw the SUV in reverse and floored it over the tree.

A Priest's Duty

"Hello, my child. I'm Father Michaelis. I am here to listen to your final words." I said as I stood behind the bars watching the man in the orange jumper.

Keith Roberts had been found guilty of premeditated murder on an outrageous level-responsible for the slaughter of 39 men, women, and children in the Locksdale shopping mall. Keith had Barricaded the doors and proceeded to stab or bludgeon everyone unfortunate enough to be locked in there with him. He'd been sentenced to death by a jury of his peers, and due to the nature of his crimes been given priority in line.

"Hello, father," Keith said with an eerie calm in his voice, his eyes never leaving the floor of his cell. "Come inside. No need to be a stranger." Keith sat on his bunk as still as a statue. His slouched figure staring a hole into the floor at his feet.

I signaled one of the guards. A buzzing echoed throughout the hall, and I proceeded inside closing the door behind me. I took a seat on the bunk opposite Keith and took in the man. He was of average height and build. Keith had a full head of hair during his trial but now was clean-shaven in preparation for the chair. It was a wonder that this small man was able to overpower so many people. Keith's bones appeared to poke out from every inch of exposed flesh. He had appeared malnourished at trial but looked closer to a skeleton than a human now.

"Are you a religious man Keith?" I asked pulling my bible out of the inner pocket of my coat. Keith looked up at me, his intense blue eyes meeting my own.

"Are you, Father?" Keith retorted, eyes still holding my own.

"Would you like me to pray for you, Keith?" I was not going to let him unnerve me. I had been doing this for quite some time. Most prisoners were relieved to give one last confession before meeting their maker while others just wanted to get one last adrenaline rush.

"Pray to who Father?" Keith smiled "My lord doesn't require prayer." Keith tilted his head and continued holding my gaze. He was waiting for a reaction from me that he was not going to get.

"I will pray to the only god there is Keith - the one true Lord." I cracked open my bible to the bookmark I kept for just this occasion.

"You think your god is still listening?" Keith let out a wild cackle at this "After centuries of life, do you honestly believe he still holds love for his creations!"

Keith threw his head back in laughter. I sat there biting my tongue waiting for the man to calm down before I continued. Keith's laughing fit finally subsided, and he once again locked eyes with me. His once piercing blue eyes had been replaced with jet-black ones.

"I've met him you know," Keith's voice had taken on a doubling quality. The slow, baritone tone had developed a deeper, evil echo just underneath it. Keith's mouth turned up into an impish grin as he continued, "Oh, it was many years ago I'd say probably seven to eight hundred years back. He's not as forgiving as your little book says he is."

"Keith, I would like to pray for you now." I broke his gaze, unsettled by what I saw reflected in his eyes. I felt his eyes searching me as I fumbled my bible in sweaty palms. Even without direct contact I could feel those black holes searching for a way into me.

"Can I tell you a secret, Father?" Keith leaned in closer covering the cramped space between us.

"Are these your final words?" I gulped trying to keep my voice from breaking.

"In this body." Keith chuckled.

"I will hear your confession," I told him, trying to keep the conversation on track.

"You ever wondered why it seems like the world is going to hell quicker and quicker?" Keith asked. "Just between you and me, Father, it's because there is a little loophole that we found. I've been doing this for quite a while, you see. Used to be, one of us could come up here take down maybe one or two of your kind before a hero would swoop in and save the day."

I met Keith's eyes, his words drawing me in.

"But your god said it best himself. The meek shall inherit the earth. And so, they did. I could walk out there right now and kill ten men before even one would stand up to me. Not to mention your laws - kill one man and stay in jail for a few years, kill two and stay in for just a little longer. It's almost like you want a form of population control." Keith roared out a laugh at this.

"Our father who art in heaven..." I started. At those words, Keith fell into an abrupt silence and narrowed his eyes in a bone-chilling glare. My voice left me.

"What makes you think he's still there?" Keith stood up and closed the distance between us.

 "While we walk free on this earth? For centuries I have walked this earth killing whoever stood in my path. It took me fifty years to come back the first time I was executed." Keith knelt still holding my eyes in his own.

"And over the years I started to realize something. Every time I was put to death, the amount of waiting it took for me to come back became less and less. The more lives I took the easier it became to take over a body." Keith grabbed the bible from my hands. A sizzling sound filled the air, and the smell of burnt flesh accompanied it.

"It took me a week to come back after my last execution." The bible burst into flames in Keith's hands.

"How long do you think it will take after all those lives, I took?"

I could hold my fear in no longer. I pounded on the iron bars as Keith cackled behind me. Within seconds guards had restrained him and ushered me out. I attended Keith's execution the next day, his blue eyes staring into mine through the two-way mirror. I watched as the doctor declared him deceased.

A week later as I was enjoying my morning coffee, I heard the thud of the newspaper hitting my door. I snatched it up quickly trying to keep the outside chill from seeping into the house. A quick glance at the front page showed a snapshot of a man in a chalk outline. It wasn't the body that had caught my attention, but the words next to it. In what I could only assume was the victim's blood, a thick red scrawl spelled out,

One day, Father.

Jingle

Mommy and Daddy always told me that I had to be asleep, or Santa wouldn't come. I always made sure I was quiet and never got up. Even when I could hear thumping or footsteps downstairs, I was a good boy. I always got the best presents every year from Santa.

Well, last night I knew I wasn't supposed to get up, but I had to. I was thirsty and Mommy forgot to give me water before bed. I knew it wasn't late, because I have a clock on my table, and my daddy taught me how to tell time. I knew Santa wouldn't be coming yet, he had too many other houses to go to before mine.

I made sure I was really quiet when I got up. Mommy always leaves my door open and a night light on in the hallway. I used to have really bad dreams, but I'm a big boy now so I don't even need the light. The floor squeaks sometimes, but it didn't last night.

I saw the light was on in the kitchen so I thought I could just ask Mommy or Daddy for some water. They weren't in there, but my favorite cup was on the counter, so I got myself some water from the fridge. Mommy likes it when I do things by myself.

I was walking back upstairs when I saw a man by our tree. I got scared because I didn't want Santa to get mad at me for being up. Santa must have been scared of me too. I know he doesn't see a lot of kids because they are always asleep.

He dropped the present he was holding when he saw me, and it made a loud *BANG* when it hit the ground.

It made me jump and I almost screamed but Santa held a finger to his lips which I know meant, "Be quiet." He stood there for a little while like that looking at me. Santa gave me a big smile and waved at me, and I waved back to him. He didn't look mad at all that I was up.

He called me by my name and told me to come over to him. He asked me why I was up, and I told him the truth. Santa wasn't mad at me and I was so happy, I didn't want all my toys to be taken away. I had so many questions for Santa, but he told me that I needed to go back to bed because it was late.

I told him I couldn't sleep because I was so excited and didn't want him to be upset with me. Santa let me have the milk we left out for him and a cookie. Then he walked me up to my room and pulled out a rag from his sack. He told me it was a special sleeping rag just in case little kids woke up when he visited.

I don't remember falling asleep, but when I woke up, I was really confused. I couldn't smell any breakfast and Mommy always makes breakfast on Christmas morning. My clock said it was eleven in the morning and we never sleep in, not even on the weekends. I must have made Santa mad.

All my presents were gone and so were my mommy and daddy. They never told me that if I saw Santa, he would take them away too. I wanted to ask them why Santa wore black clothes now instead of red. I wanted to ask mommy and daddy why Santa had a knife.

****

I patted the kid on the back and ruffled his hair. I placed my pad with the case notes back into my pocket as I stood up and motioned for the case worker. As I got to my cruiser, I lit a cigarette and breathed a sigh of relief. I waved one more time at the kid as I slid into the cruiser. I studied his face as he waved back waiting to see if he recognized me.

Unplug

I just needed to unplug for a little while. To get away from everything. The noise of the city, the droning of my coworkers, and the constant odors that come along with people. It all needed to go away.

A cabin by the lake in the off-season. What better way to rid myself of unwanted stimuli than no stimuli? I told my boss of my plans to make sure I could go ahead and book the cabin. He was very understanding and the day before my vacation he slipped me a small box.

"Use this," He suggested. "It's something my doctor gave me a while back. An ambient noise machine might help you sleep at night. Take care of yourself out there Michael."

Pine needles snapped underfoot as a cold breeze blew more onto the path. Path wasn't the right word for it - just a rough line with slightly less pine needle coverage led from the parking area. The trees swayed slightly from a newer stronger breeze.

For the first time in ages, my shoulders sagged, and my brow relaxed. The silence engulfed me as I stood there basking in the early morning rays. I threw my aging sea bag onto my shoulders. The smell of its rough plastic brought back long-forgotten memories of simpler times.

Being told where to go and when to go. What to eat and when to eat it. When to shoot and when to be at ease. Much simpler times back then, before life had come crashing in.

The cabin was a small, withered husk of what the pictures had shown. A dilapidated porch complete with a swing held on by only one chain framed the screen door. The swing rocked back and forth scraping the porch and breaking the silence. The steps creaked and groaned not used to supporting weight other than their own.

I held onto hope as I pulled open the rickety screen door. Sure, Father Time and Mother Nature'd had their way with the exterior, but the insides had to be better. The front door stuck fast as I turned the knob in both directions. I leaned my shoulder into the center of the door and pushed off against the sagging porch.

The door finally gave way, along with the board I had been using as a foot prop sending me headfirst onto the hardwood floor. Mildew and decay filled my nostrils. The cabin floor rustled as I got my feet under me. The door had swung back shut from the force of my entry, causing the cabin to be swallowed up by darkness.

The floor rustled even more as I backed my way up to where I remembered the door being. Splinters poked and prodded my skin as I searched for a light switch. A rustling came from the far side of the room while my hand groped for a light switch. Panic set in at the sound, and I couldn't let go of the possibility of a bear hibernating in an abandoned cabin.

I dropped my hands to my side trying to quiet myself when I felt the object, I had grabbed from my glove compartment earlier. The cabin was illuminated by the beam of the flashlight I had stashed in my pocket. A plump raccoon tottered along the wall directly ahead of me, probably awoken by my loud entrance during his nap time. It stared at the light for a moment and waddled toward the open window.

The lights hummed to life slowly. The switch was a lot easier to find with the flashlight beam. The interior of the cabin wasn't quite as bad as its outward appearance. The mildew smell I had been bathed in earlier came from a pile of leaves the raccoon must have brought in through the open window. Once the window was closed and I had a fire going I inspected the rest of the cabin.

The bedroom, while stale smelling and typical, would be a fine place to sleep. The kitchen held the little necessities I would need for a weekend retreat. The bathroom was a step above an outhouse but was at least functional and inside. I sat my bag down next to the bed, kicked off my boots, and flopped down onto the sinking mattress.

I pulled the ambient noise machine out of my pack and placed it on the dusty nightstand. It resembled a typical portable CD player. It had a simple on-and-off switch with a dial to go between different noises. I flipped it over and saw a large compartment for batteries and a power cord tucked into a slot on the side. Laying the device back down I set about unpacking my meager possessions.

The waves rippled across the lake lapping against the shoreline. I stared out along the expanse, as I rested my back against a tree stump about ten feet or so from the shore. This far into winter, all creatures that could have disturbed my relaxation were deep in hibernation. I sat there motionless for hours just taking in the calm.

Once the chill had crept in too far for my liking, I headed back to the cabin. For being as old as it was the cabin held the heat from the fire very well. I fixed myself a bowl of canned soup and relaxed in the wooden rocking chair. The crackling of the flames and a full stomach worked magic on my already tired mind.

"Michael!" A familiar voice shouted, shaking me wide awake. "Michael Darius Tucker, you answer me when I am speaking to you!"

My hands shot up instinctively to my face shielding it from the slap that had always followed those words. I wiped the sleep from my eyes and stared around the brightly lit cabin. My mother's voice had not had a place in my dreams for a very long time. Her voice hadn't had a place among the living for even longer.

"YOU WILL ANSWER ME, MICHAEL!"

The voice blared from seemingly every corner of the cabin. The savageness of its tone shook me so hard that I fell out of my chair, my hand grazing the fireplace as I tried to soften my fall. I scrambled to my feet holding my hand to my chest, the burning sensation clearing my head. I looked around the cabin trying to spot a figure or speaker - anything to explain the voice.

"Wrong again, Michael." The voice scolded. "You know what happens to little boys when they don't respond to adults, right?"

I instinctively rubbed my cheek. Memories of the pain I had experienced all too often resurfacing.

"Why don't you come in here." The voice urged sweetly. "Have a little chat with your dear old mother, Michael?"

Malice had been replaced with kindness and at a quieter volume, I could finally pinpoint where the voice was coming from. As I cautiously walked into the bedroom, my body was tense ready to pounce. I was ready to protect myself from whoever had snuck in. I scanned the room, looking into every darkened corner.

"Come now, Michael," The voice sneered. "I raised you to be smarter than that didn't I? Or did the beatings I gave you not sink in deep enough?"

The voice came out plaintively from the ambient noise machine. I stared at it for a moment trying to figure out if I was still dreaming or not. I walked over to the machine and flipped the switch to the off position. Dream or not my mother has no place in it.

"It's not a dream Michael," the voice spat. "Your hand should be answer enough for that. I guess I failed you as a mother, all those hard-taught lessons didn't stick."

I whirled around back to the device. The switch was still set to the off position, yet the voice had come through its speaker. I flipped it onto its side and opened the battery compartment. I dumped all the batteries from it. I watched as the red light faded away on the front of the device. Once it had disappeared, I turned to head back to the living room the heat had become too stifling.

"Are you going to walk away from me when I'm talking to you, Michael?" the voice called out.

I whirled around at the sound of the voice. The red power indicator light was once again illuminated.

"I'm hurt, Michael," The voice pouted. "First, you don't show up to my funeral and now you can't even be bothered to listen to me as I'm speaking to you from beyond death. You were always an ungrateful little shit."

I backed away colliding with the cabin wall. The pain in my hand and the splinter driving into my back proved to me how real this was. She had been dead for three years now I verified her body at the morgue. I had given the funeral director everything he'd needed to bury her.

"I'm still waiting on you to speak, Michael," The voice was losing its patience. "You know mother doesn't like to be kept waiting."

I could hear crackling. I spotted the antenna on the top of the machine. Someone was broadcasting this! Some sick fuck out there was hijacking the signal and broadcasting this just for me.

"You're dead!" I cried out. "I should know mother - I'm the one that fired the gun."

I dove at the machine ready to pull the plug from the wall. My burnt hand groped behind the nightstand trying to locate the cord only to see it tucked firmly in its holder.

"You never plugged it in Michael." I could see her rolling her eyes in my mind. You were always a forgetful little brat."

Sweat dripped off my forehead. The temperature in the cabin was rising by the second.

"You're not real!" I screamed at the machine as I threw it at the door. A maniacal cackle blasted through the speakers filling the room. "I buried you!"

"What's your FUCKING POINT!" The voice shrieked. "I'm right here, Michael! Back to teach you one final FUCKING LESSON!"

I ran to the door. My injured hand flared in pain from the heat of the doorknob.

"Are you ready for your lesson Michael?"

"Fuck you, you dead BITCH!" I screamed.

Flames and smoke hit me as soon as I opened the door. The oxygen that had been sealed in with me ignited, robbing me of breath immediately. The living room was engulfed in flames. A post from the ceiling had fallen blocking the doorway.

"Never leave a fireplace unattended Michael." The voice sang. "You never know when a log can roll out. I'll be seeing you soon. Mother can't wait to give you a big hug."

Her cackle warbled in and out as the speakers melted.

My Place

"It's perfect!" I shouted to the realtor.

"So, you're going to put an offer down?" she responded with almost equal excitement.

"Whatever they want I'll pay it, hell I'll write a check right now!" I exclaimed.

A month later I had signed the final paper, and the keys were handed over. After a week of back-breaking work I was officially living in my place. I teach literature at Price college, and while this was far from my dream job it afforded me the luxury of tenure. No more leasing, no more scummy landlords dragging their feet on maintenance, and no more noisy neighbors.

I could finally concentrate and enjoy some me time, I could finish my books, and I could even write that script I've been working on for the last few years. It wasn't the biggest house in the world, but the office with built-in wall-to-wall bookshelves had me hooked the moment I saw it. I spent the last few days of my vacation unpacking and setting things right until that wonderful Monday morning alarm rang out.

With classes back in session I got myself back into my old routine easily - a little coffee, some eggs, and two slices of toast in my office with the morning sun warming my back. I spent the next few weeks going through the motions at school, but all I wanted was to be back at my desk in my office. After weeks of teaching, slack-jawed party animals came the glorious winter break. My entire plan for the holiday consisted of sitting at my desk with a book or two and getting my fireplace in working order.

Day one of the break was a standard ordeal. I did the usual morning routine and spent the rest of my day lost in my book until the winter chill crept in. I had some wood delivered the week before; and as the sun set, I went about getting the fireplace ready. Once I got the logs set, I tried the flue only to find it stuck tight. After a few minutes of wrestling with the latch, it came loose, and a soot-covered book fell. Soot billowed out around the forgotten item.

I put the book aside and got the fire going. My warmth was more important than a mysterious book. I sat down as the fire started fighting the chill and dusted off the cover of the book. It was an unremarkable book, with a simple black cover, no title, and no markings at all. The only words in the book were the title *My Place*. I flipped through it a few times to find a name or anything that might point out where the book had come from and why it had been hidden away.

The glow from the fire cast long shadows across the room and the book. I decided it was time to relax with my own book and enjoy my newfound warmth. Sleep found me shortly after.

The next day started the same as the other except for my stiff back from the couch. I spent the morning in my office chair with a heat pack pressed firmly into my back. I searched through my collection of books hoping to find something I hadn't already read a few times over. Glancing through my collection of Greek mythology, I spotted the book from the chimney. I pulled it out trying to remember when I had placed it on the shelf.

The light of the sun did nothing to help the appearance of the book. It still held the same blank cover and cover with soot marking. I opened the book up again to see the same title *My Place*. Directly below that scrawled in the same black ink the words "*It's not yours*" were written. The lines differed greatly; the title was written in fluid light letters, while the latter was written hard and forced as if the handwriting it had trouble grasping the pen.

I wondered to myself if my sleeping situation might have caused me to sleepwalk and place the book on the shelf. Sleepwalking or not I distinctly remember there only being a title on the pages. I placed the book down on the desk. My back had begun to feel better, and it was time to get to enjoying my day.

After busying myself around the house for most of the afternoon I came upon a very troubling discovery. Sleeping anywhere other than the den was out of the question. I had kept the fire going throughout the day, but its warmth didn't pass over the threshold.

I laid down on the couch bundled in blankets hoping to combat the stiff back before it formed. The fire crackled and popped as I turned the book over in my hands. I repeated the words over and over again in my head. *It's my place not yours, it's my place not yours, it's my place not yours.* Eventually the warmth of the fire and blankets carried me off to sleep. I dreamt of whispers coming from the flue.

The sounds of busy streets woke me from a fitful sleep of hushed voices. I dragged myself off the couch and into the outside air hoping to wake myself up. People avoided me on the street seeming to assume I was drunk or strung out.

It wasn't until I walked into the bookstore down the street that I realized why they had been avoiding me.

I grabbed a newspaper from the rack to catch up on daily events only to cover the page in ashen fingerprints. Profusely apologizing to the clerk and handing them some wadded up bills, I quickly made my way back to my place. I was covered in soot from head to toe.

After a good scrubbing I managed to transfer the soot all over the shower instead of myself. Feeling refreshed and whole again I made my way back to the bookstore and purchased a leather-bound blank book. I had plans of starting to write my own manuscript and trusted pen and paper more than computer programs.

The chill had settled into the house earlier than before, forcing me into the den again. As the fire warmed me and whispered to me through its pops and cracks. I noticed my books had become disorganized again. The blank book had now found itself between Dickens and Stoker. Grabbing the book deposited a fresh layer of ash on my hands.

The book also left a considerable amount of ash on the trash bag I placed it in. After washing up and placing the bag on the stoop I decided it was time to relax and fill my stomach. My tv dinner and blanket did nothing against the cold kitchen. I made a note to myself to call someone the next morning to come check out the building.

The couch was calling my name. I needed warmth and I wanted nothing more than to fall asleep with a good book in my hands. I found an old favorite of mine and settled down. The book fell apart in my hands as soon as I opened it up. Pages had been shredded to ribbons, words had been scratched out, and the spine had been broken.

I threw the blankets off of me and searched the house. Someone had clearly done this, but why would they break in just to destroy an old book? All the locks were still in place and all the windows were still shut tight. As I returned to the den, I noticed the old book sitting open on my coffee table. Its pages now open to display in large, scratched letters *LEAVE NOW.*

I didn't sleep. Every time I closed my eyes, I kept hearing *My place it's not yours. Never will be. LEAVE NOW* repeated over and over. In my sleep deprived state, I swore I had seen soot covered hands coming from the chimney. I tried calling the original owners once the sun had risen, but just got a disconnected tone. The realtor ignored my calls and blocked me after the third try.

I couldn't put myself through another night like that. I tried going to the realtor's office, but the building showed no signs of being in use. When I got back to my house, I found everything in ruin. Furniture had been toppled over, dishes broken on the floor, and clothes thrown everywhere. I tried calling the police, but I couldn't get a bar of service anywhere in the house.

The cold was too much to handle and forced me into the den. The fire blazed in its hearth. I armed myself with the fireplace poker in case the person responsible was still here. As I straightened up, I brushed against the mantle and knocked off the book.

I remember putting it outside in the trash the night before so how could it have possibly made it onto the mantle? Opening it up I saw the pages had been filled in completely now. Line after line, page after page full of the same writings.

It's my place not yours! It never will be LEAVE NOW!

Hundreds of pages all bearing the same hard scrawling handwriting. The fire warmed my back and cast uneasy shadows on the book as I thumbed it to the end. The final page held only two words that took up the entirety of the page.

Last chance

I tossed the book into the fire. As soon as it touched the flame screams roared and shook the room. I dropped the poker trying to cover my ears. Black hands emerged from the top of the chimney and latched onto my wrists.

"I warned you,"

****
****

"Didn't we just sell this place?"

"Look all I know is this guy called and said he wants to sell and told me where to send the check. Everyone that buys this place does it within the first year at least."

"Doesn't that seem a bit odd to you?"

"What part of thirty percent of sales price seems odd to you? We make a profit they sell cheap and buy cheap. Now let's get this place ready."

"It's smokey in here maybe the chimney is messed up."

"It's the flue. Guy probably tried to start a fire after I told him not to the place has central heating. I've had to clean that damn chimney out so many times I finally just sealed it off. Birds and animals would get in and burn up. Used to find all these bone shards and the place would stink to high heaven for a while."

"Yeah, I can smell it alright. Let's come back tomorrow. Just leave a window open."

The Joys of Time Travel

I grabbed the mail from the post man and ushered him on his way. I shuffled through the pile rapidly stopping on one with a familiar scrawl. I pushed the envelope aside. There are more important things to do today than reading the mail. I've done it, I've finally perfected my device. All of space and time are right here at my fingertips! Years of research and sleepless nights have all led me to where I stand today.

My colleagues have all laughed at me and told me this was impossible. But, once I see and experience all that I've ever dreamed of I shall appear at their house in twenty, nay - thirty years! They will be old and decrepit while I retain my youth and shove my adventures down their throats. Now I just need to decide where to go first.

I could go see the eruption of Pompeii. Watch as the pyramids were built and see the magnificence of their creation. I could even go see the creation of the universe and answer the questions that have plagued us all for eons!

I could witness the future of the human race and bring back inventions that would set me and my family for life. I really couldn't though - that would create a paradox and even rupture the universe. I have to make it count. I have to go to one time and place and make it count. In the chance that something goes wrong, I have to make my first voyage worth the risk.

I know what I'll do! I'll go to the very end of time. I'll see what happens to the world and see when it takes place. The ability to see the entirety of everything blink out of existence is well worth the risk.

The machine hums to life as I switch on the controls. My pen and paper stand at the ready to record all that I see. I turn the dials as far as they will go, hoping it's enough to take me to where I intend. With hope and prayer, I push the button propelling me to sights and times unknown.

It is glorious! All of space is displayed before me, with not a planet in sight, save for a dying star. The fortified glass allows me a perfect view of my surroundings and I am in awe. The vast emptiness expands in every direction. What once was a beautiful galaxy now stood as empty as a fresh canvas. I admire the works of the universe before curiosity strikes me.

I have to know just how far ahead I have gone. I adjust the dials to see and proceed to calculate how many eons I must have flown through. Twenty thousand years is all it took to get to the end of the universe! So fleeting is life once you can see the end of it all.

My hubris will be the death of me one day I'm sure of it. I want to see how it happens. I start rewinding the dials slowly making my way back through the years. I can see space debris pieces of planets left over from their collapse.

I have rewound ten thousand years and I still can't find the moment. Surely our universe has more than ten thousand years left to it. Another five thousand and more and more debris is lingering. Surely, I have to be getting closer!

A fool! I have been an ignorant fool. I have rewound the dials so many times searching for the exact moment. I still cannot find it and now have drained the power of my craft.

My instruments or calculations can't be right. I have rewound to the day after I left and can find nothing.

I must have made a mistake - an error in calculations somewhere. I'm going to use my pen and paper and create a letter for myself. I know it will mess with the timeline, but I have to warn myself not to go down this path. I have just enough power left to send a letter back and hope my past self reads it.

Thin Spots

Has the world ever just felt off?

Your vision disorients, your skin prickles, and your mind goes fuzzy?

Is it random?

Or is it in select areas?

I've come to see the world for what it is. Our world is, for lack of better words, thin. Imagine wrapping some haphazard sculpture in cheap dollar-store wrapping paper. One wrong prod and you see what lies underneath.

Most enjoy their days ignorant of the inner workings of our world, while others live with it glaring them in the face day by day. We even make special places in society for them. I used to ignore it. I used to just shake off the feelings of the thin spots, but I learned that the things on the other side can sometimes poke back. The veil isn't just flimsy on our side.

It was my stay in a cabin that brought me in contact with that paper-like veil for the first time. It was a beautiful cabin surrounded by tall pines and hills for miles around. I rented it out to get a little peace and quiet from my daily life.

The moment I entered the cabin my body knew something was off. Every synapse in my brain shouted at me to run. I brushed it off. It had to just be nerves about staying in an unknown place for the first time. I unloaded my baggage and went about exploring the surroundings.

After a tiring hike, food and shelter were calling for me. I got the fire going and warmed up my scant meal on the stovetop. The view from the windows was beautiful. I admired the trees waving in the wind framed by the waning sun. It was odd but the wind must have come up as I came back in from my hike. There hadn't been so much as a breeze while I was out. A cold chill shot through my spine and as I reached up to close the window my fingers brushed against what I could only describe as a sheet of plastic.

I decided to take my supper outside. I couldn't shake the feeling inside the cabin. As I enjoyed my meal of canned soup and the serenity of nature, it hit me just how still everything suddenly was. I peered back into the cabin and saw it - the trees in the windows were heaving back and forth, but the ones in front of me were deathly still. That's when I finally caught why I felt so wrong here - I hadn't heard a single sound since I'd arrived.

No animals had made a single noise, no gust of wind could be heard, no snapping branches, no acorns fell, no rustle of leaves or falling pebbles resounding nearby or in the distance. I went back inside. The woods started to unnerve me even more than the inside did. I stared out the windows at the swaying trees and fading sunlight. It became unsettling to experience one thing while a few feet away through a looking glass a completely opposite thing was happening outside. I decided to open the window.

Heat and sulfur hit me as the breath was ripped from my body. I pulled the frame down as quickly as I could and sliced my palm on a sliver of wood. The blood flowed freely, but not towards the ground - it swayed in the air and floated towards the window. Darkness descended upon the windows while sunlight shone under the door. Nothing was making sense anymore.

I walked to the bathroom and bandaged my hand up. I didn't need to pass out from blood loss. Not here. The windows once again showed trees rippling in the breeze and the descending sun. My skin prickled, and my vision blurred. I couldn't stay here anymore. I had to go. I had to go now.

I grabbed my bags and headed for the door. The only light in the cabin came from the now dwindling fireplace. The windows had gone black again. I could suddenly hear the first sounds since I entered the cabin - branches scraping the side of the building. My eyes were fixated on the windows. They'd started to pulsate and squirm. The inky blackness started to move.

My mind screamed at me to run! Run now! Move! Do something! I couldn't tear my gaze from the window. My body was rooted to the spot, bags hanging limply from my hands. I tried to make sense of it - how could I see daylight from the door frame and absolute night from the windows? A pair of ember red eyes emerged through the darkness and burned into mine.

When they blinked, my body finally decided to listen to me. I ran to the door and busted through it. Daylight and wind hit me as soon as I cleared the threshold. I didn't stop running until I was safely in the car with the doors locked.

I looked around before starting the engine. The windows were unobstructed all through the cabin. The trees were a good 50 feet from the cabin, and all saplings at that. I couldn't have seen what I knew I saw I couldn't have heard what I knew I heard. I threw the car in reverse and got the hell out of there.

I now have a nice long scar on my palm to remember that trip by now. I've joined online chats and message threads related to events like these and the one thing I've learned is our world is thin. All it takes is a little push or prod to open it up, but we aren't the only ones that can push. Once you've stared into that other side it's a lot easier to notice it again. It's a lot easier for it to notice you, too.

Watch the reflections and the windows listen for sounds or the lack of them and when your mind tells you to run just run.

The Pharmacist

"I'm glad you could drop in. I figured you were on the way. Oh, how tired you must be. I made a pot of tea and I made it strong just for you."

"Do you know why I'm here?"

"Oh yes! I have an inkling, but can you oblige an old man to reminisce for a short while."

"Make it quick, I want to finish this nasty business soon."

My father built this funeral home from the ground up wanting to pass it down to his family. He trained me in all the necessities, receiving the body, cleaning it up, dressing it, and preparing it for longevity. I learned it all from a young age. My days were simple; wake up, go to school, go to the funeral home, help my father, and go to sleep again.

It was during this time I found a love for chemistry and anatomy. My father taught me all about how to make embalming fluid. How to mix formaldehyde, methanol, and glutaraldehyde. How to fix the bodies correctly while also teaching me about the body's structure and different organs' purposes.

It came as quite a shock to him when I told him I would be going to college instead of taking over the funeral home.

"Are you close to finishing? The tea is good, but the night is slipping, and my bed is calling."

"Yes, my apologies short stories turn into novels as you age."

I finished my education with a Bachelor of Science. Chemistry and anatomy being my primary sources of study. I bummed around for a while until I landed a job with a pharmacist who was as ready to teach as I was ready to learn. Life went on, I learned what I could from him and eventually ran the pharmacy when he came to retirement age. Once he passed away, I took ownership and hired another gentleman like myself and repeated the deed that had been done for me.

A phone call came that threw my life off track; my father had been hospitalized. It was not so much of a shock he was well on in age, a chain smoker, and a drunk. When I went to visit him, he looked worse off than the bodies he had spent the last forty years prepping for their long slumber. He was in pain; lung cancer was already eating away at what was left of his miserable body. All he wanted was to finish out his days at home. It took a bit of paperwork but with my knowledge they allowed me to take him home.

Hasty arrangements were made, the pharmacy dealt with, and I sold my home to move into the old family home. I settled in easily and went to work at the funeral parlor. Luckily business was slow, and I could focus on my father's health.

"Can we please speed this up? You said you would make this short."

"Very well I'll skip over some parts."

My father was deteriorating rapidly but the doctors gave him another six months. Bunch of hacks they were you could see death's hand gripping his shoulder. I decided mercy was the better option for him. He wasn't a bad man, and six months of pain wasn't justice for him. I racked my brain for a way to help him. Without much wait, it came to me. A clear, simple, and easy way to help him along. He passed easily and after the funeral, I did the work myself. It's what he wanted; I was left in a peculiar situation - I had run of both the pharmacy and funeral home.

A smart man would've sold the funeral home due to a lack of business, but a wise man would see the potential in having both.

"Just tell me how you did it so this can be over." A yawn broke up the man's speech.

Well, like I said - it was clear and simple and easy. You find the people who were on the, let's say, "last-mile medicines." The ones that made them comfortable instead of curing, and you pay them a house visit. Offer them a way out with no pain. The only condition is that I do the funeral. No autopsies due to their health - not like it would matter either way.

"You're not looking so good, inspector. Was the tea not to your liking?"

"I'm just a little weak - my head is killing me."

"Ah, yes that would be the insulin kicking in. You have to put in quite a bit to take down a healthy person of your size. Strong tea helps mask the smell."

"Why…why would you do this?"

"Why to you? Or why at all?" Both are pointless questions if you use half your brain, Detective."

Thud

Poor boy won't get his answer, but oh well. I can finish the tale for you, my ever-so-clever friend. You found me just before him. If he had walked in on me dealing with you, well, I dare say I'd be the one on the ground now.

I've been talking for a while now and honestly; I've grown tired of this. My fascination with anatomy wasn't for the dead but for the living. It took so long but after practicing over the last few years, I've found the perfect chemical mix to keep you calm even while I cut you open. I've managed to keep some alive for three hours while severing individual tendons. It's a good thing they all requested closed - caskets I couldn't repair everything.

Owning a funeral home has its perks when it comes to covering up evidence. I honestly figured I'd have been caught long ago, but the old pharmacist was a great mentor. Just think - if you had made it here slightly later and had been a bit more careful, you'd be the most renowned journalist in the state. Instead, let's see if I can break my own record and go for four hours this time.

Cucuy

*(The Cucuy (*Koo-Kwee*), otherwise known as Coco, is a mythical being with ties to Spain and Portugal. It is believed that Cucuy would kidnap and eat misbehaving children. There are many varying legends surrounding this mythical entity.)*

The doorbell rang out and I rushed to the door, my slippers popping against the hardwood. The doorknob sat cold in my hand as the doorbell rang again, I turned the knob and put on my biggest smile. Jenna stood shivering in the late day sun. The Winter wind blew in small flurries of snow between the two of us.

"Hey Jenna…"

I trailed off nervously as Jenna brushed me aside and dropped her stuff next to the couch. Jenna and I used to be best friends, but I guess middle school has a way of changing people. We had been next door neighbors since kindergarten. Our moms had become best friends through our incessant need for play dates.

"Hey, Stacy where's your mom?" Jenna's mom darted inside and closed the door behind her, forcing the cold back out.

"Kitchen," I said and went to sit back down on the couch. Jenna was doing her best to look as miserable as possible. She glanced at me a made a disgusted face and returned her attention to the loose strand on her blue jeans. The clock hands ticked by in the silence of the living room, neither of us trying to break it. As I settled in and pressed play on the TV remote, I could hear some of the conversations between our moms.

"Thank you for doing this." Jenna's mom choked on her words slightly I could hear the scuffle of my mom's slippers as she went to her. There were some very quiet sobs and then Mom hushed her.

"You have to be strong." Mom whispered. "I've got Jenna for as long as you need me to."

Jenna snatched the remote and turned up the TV, drowning out the rest of the conversation. I heard a sniffle escape from her before the tv volume reached its peak. Jenna's mom came out a little later, hugged Jenna hard, and left quickly to keep the cold air out.

"Girls," Mom yelled from the kitchen. "Go play for a little while; I'm getting supper ready."

"Let's go," I said standing up from the couch. Jenna stayed seated and started flipping through the tv channels. I cleared my throat and waited patiently by the staircase. With one final sigh she turned the tv off and headed upstairs. She dragged her feet and flopped down on the bed as soon as we got in.

"This is bullshit" Jenna hissed at me.

I clenched my fist and listened for footsteps from the kitchen sure my mother had heard her. Jenna never used to swear. We used to find creative ways around the words that our mom's and Dad's had blurted out. Swearing was not allowed in this house.

"Jenna you can't talk like that." I stammered out, fists still clenched. My throat dry from confronting her.

"Oh yeah?" Jenna snorted back a laugh. "And what is the baby going to do about it huh?"

Jenna stood and stared down at me. Same age or not Jenna had always looked down on me. She had hit her growth spurt earlier than me and even when I hit my own, she was still several inches taller than me. Jenna had it all. She was tall, thin, had beautiful straight hair. That's what made the popular kids notice her. The popular group didn't want me around and Jenna had made sure I understood that.

 "Please Jenna." I gulped, pushing down my tears. I balled my fists and stared straight back into her cold blue eyes. "I don't want to make my mom mad, and she doesn't like that language."

My mind screamed at me to back down, remembering the pain she had inflicted on me before. Jenna broke eye contact first, retreating a step back from me. In all our years together she had been the ringleader with me as the dancing monkey. I could never tell her no or argue. She balled her fist and raised it at my eye level quickly. When I didn't flinch, Jenna sat back down on the bed and glared at me.

 "Guess the baby found her backbone finally." Jenna leaned against the wall.

"We used to be friends Jenna what happened?" I tried to redirect the conversation as I leaned against the wall opposite her, trying to meet her eyes.

"You already know what happened." She muttered, twirling the same loose string from her jeans again.

A loud thud came from out in the hallway.

"What was that?" Jenna asked, narrowing her eyes at the door.

"Old house," I shrugged. "Something probably fell off the wall."

"Stacy." Jenna said softly, almost making me believe she might care. "That sounded bad are you sure your mom is fine?"

"I've made new friends you know, and they like me and play with me!" I yelled at her.

"Girls," my mom shouted, "Is everything okay up there?"

"Yeah, Mom everything's fine," I shouted down to her.

Jenna sat on the bed, arms crossed, glaring at me, daring me to try baring my fangs at her again. I had never stood up to Jenna before and my short-lived burst of adrenaline had been shattered by mom's intervention. Silence lingered in the air between us until another loud thud rang out and Jenna jumped to her feet.

"Girls," Mom shouted at us with agitation in her voice. "Quit playing around and come eat."

I started downstairs with Jenna. She stopped outside my door and turned toward the guest room. Mom called for us again, Jenna stomped in frustration and followed me downstairs. Supper was eaten in silence with mom looking between the both of us. Mom tried to start a conversation once, but realized from Jenna's look she wasn't going to be very talkative.

After supper was finished and the kitchen cleaned Jenna and I got ready for bed. Jenna had the guest room since Mom said we were too big to share a room anymore. After getting dressed and saying goodnight to mom, I made my way to the guest room. Jenna sat on the edge of the bed and made a quick swiping motion at her eyes when I came in.

"What do you want?" She demanded.

"I want to talk," I said easing the door closed behind me.

"Yeah well, I don't," Jenna crossed her arms and stared at the wall.

"This is the last chance we have so I just want to get it all out, Jenna." I explained.

"What do you mean last," Jenna turned to me, her eyebrows raised.

"Shut up," I spat at her. "You know what? It's your turn to listen!"

Venom was dripping from each word. I had held this in for too long. My hands were clenched at my sides and my legs were shaking, I needed to say this before it was too late.

"You have been so mean to me for so long Jenna why?" Tears were creeping in but not from sadness. "What did I ever do to you besides be your friend?"

"Oh, Psh, what," Jenna sputtered, arguing just to argue. "Like you've been such a great friend?"

"All those times you put gum on my seat?" I asked not giving her time to continue. "All those rumors you spread about me?"

"They were just jokes Stacy, calm down." Jenna started to get up to confront me.

"Sit down!" I commanded. The timing wasn't right, and I could see those red eyes under the bed just waiting for their chance. I took a deep breath reminding myself to be quiet.

"They weren't jokes Jenna I had to go to therapy for all the stuff you did to me!" I paused to wipe away a stray tear. "They put me on so much medication! You tortured me and left me with no friends. No one would even look at me after the rumors."

Jenna sat motionless on the bed; knees curled up to her chest. Her eyes had turned watery. She had made herself as small as possible against the wall.

"I'm sorry Stacy." Jenna sobbed. "I only did that because of what I was going through with my mom and -"

"Too fucking late Jenna," I locked the door behind me and slowly made my way over to the bed. Jenna's eye went wide with fear. She had never seen me stand up to her before. "I made a new friend you see, and he isn't mean to me."

A low growl came from beneath the bed. Jenna kept her eyes locked on mine. I smiled at her showing as many of my teeth as I could, just like my friend taught me. Jenna whimpered and beneath the bed the low growl turned into a slow cackle.

"Do you want to meet my friend?" I stopped a few feet from the bed and stared at the darkness below the sheets. "He said he's been dying to meet you."

Claws tear at the floorboards as my friend, Cucuy, pulls himself out from under the bed. He's very tall and somehow manages to fit himself under my bed or in my closet. His red eyes shine down on me and his mouth splits into a wide grin. His teeth are very sharp, but his smile is a very happy one. He told me he had a very special place for girls like Jenna and that when he's done, she won't be mean to me anymore.

"Stacy, what is that!" Jenna starts to scream but Cucuy wraps a clawed hand around her mouth and drags her out the window before she can utter another sound. I leave the window open in case he comes back and needs a place to sleep. I tip toe to the door and look down the hallway. Making sure the coast is clear I tip toe back to my room and doze off as soon as my head lands on the pillow.

Mom woke me up in the morning shaking me. It took me a little while to understand her while still half asleep.

"Where is Jenna!" Mom was shouting at me.

"Oh," I yawned and sat up as my consciousness came back to me. "it's okay Mom - Mr. Cucuy took her last night to help her be a better person. He said he will bring her back soon and she can be my friend again."

I smiled at her. I was so happy knowing my friend would come back to me in a few days. My mom just stared into my eyes shock displayed on her face. Her eyes searched the room looking for any clue of what was going on. Her gaze came to rest on my nightstand. My mother's face fell, and tears began to well in her eyes.

"Stacy, Baby, I need you to answer me honestly." She lowered her voice and directed her gaze at me. I noticed something red at the bottom of her robe, it looked kind of sticky, like she had stepped in jelly. My gaze slowly wandering from her robe to the nightstand she had been staring at. My eyes taking in the bloody knife and the Halloween mask.

"Stacy, look at me!" Her voice rising to a shrill pitch. "When is the last time you took your medicine?!"

A Damn Good Doctor

"You know, a good doctor is hard to come by nowadays, Ms. Johnson." I said, fanning the paperwork in my hands.

"I know." Ms. Johnson replied, fidgeting in her seat. "The work is a bit scary."

"Oh, no need to be scared - everything is perfectly controlled and standard." I leaned back in my chair and showed the multitude of pictures displayed on the wall. "All these women came to me asking for my help and, like any good doctor, I helped them."

"But can you fix my issue?" she asked skeptically. "The other doctors said they wouldn't touch it."

"Psh," I waved my hand dismissively. "A bunch of tight asses. They are more worried about lawsuits and their numbers than they are about helping their patients.

"Just give this a look-over." I rifled through the papers on my desk and handed her the waiver form. "Once you're ready we can get everything started."

She clasped the paper in a death grip and scanned the words. Without even so much as a cursory glance, she laid the paper down and signed it in a big swirling script.

"There," she said with confidence. "I don't care what the cost is or what happens I just want you to help me."

"And that I shall do ma'am," I promised. "Now tell me again what the exact issue is and what you would like me to do about it."

"I have a lump here at the back of my neck." She pulled her hair to the side to give me a clear view. "It's obscene, and I would like it removed. The others refuse to work on it saying that it's a risk to my safety."

"I assure you I've reviewed the x-rays sent over by the doctors." I told her with a sympathetic smile. "And there is no cause to worry. It will be an inpatient treatment and once I'm done you will no longer have to worry about it."

"I knew I could count on you doctor." She exclaimed gratefully. "When can we start?"

"I'm quite booked but I think we can fit you in tomorrow afternoon," I glanced down at my calendar, checking over it one more time. "How does that sound?"

"Do I need to do anything?" She asked.

"Standard practice is no food or drinks after midnight and no medicines," I explained. "Wouldn't want it to mess with the anesthesia."

Ms. Johnson left the room giddy as a schoolgirl. While I admired the before and after photos of my life's handiwork, I mused about the blank check neatly tucked away for tonight's deposit.

The next morning was full of minor cosmetic surgeries. I had entered into the practice as a gag. Plastic surgery was not a respectable way for a doctorate to gain money. But you treat the right amount of people the right way, and oh the doors that unlock for you. What had started as a joke had turned into a very lucrative practice.

I was a damn good doctor, and I took care of any problems my clients had. For the right amount of money, of course. Some were not considered ethical, but I looked after my clients, and they looked after me in kind.

Ms. Johnson came in all smiles. Her beaming was contagious as she passed the receptionist to me.

"All ready, Doctor." She announced gleefully.

"Good to hear ma'am," I replied. "Now let's get you all settled in and ready to go."

The procedure went smoothly. The other doctors were correct in their assumptions. The tumor at the base of her skull was a significant risk to her health. Thankfully, the document she signed releasing me of any liability should the surgery go awry was safely tucked away.

As I laid her on the slab and covered her up with the sheet, I thought back to the many people I had helped over the years. The countless mob bosses who needed some competition silenced. The high-profile lawyers who needed a mistress dealt with. Or the rich husbands whose ex-wives were going to get a big fat check.

Mr. Johnson had come to see me a few days before his soon-to-be ex-wife. He knew she was set to get most of his money and other assets once their divorce was finalized. One of my old clients had referred him to me and had assured him of my usefulness. All I needed to do was get her booked in for an appointment before the trial date.

My secretary just so happened to receive her number from one of Ms. Johnson's previous doctors. Or at least that's what I told her to tell Ms. Johnson. Mr. Johnson's blank check would have to wait a while to be cashed. I couldn't risk anyone nosy enough to investigate noticing a sizeable payment being deposited shortly after her death. Like I said, I'm a damn good doctor.

Looking Back

The starry night sky has always fascinated me. Laying in the field and looking up at the infinity of space would always bring out the scientist in me. I used to wonder to myself just what those shining lights were hiding in their majesty. So of course, what other path was there for me but to be an astronomer?

After years of study and interning, I was hired at a small laboratory. My laminated name card displayed the words, "Dr. David Rose," proudly. I was in love from the moment I set foot inside the facility.

We were by no means a fancy observatory like the Gemini or Keck. Our equipment was dated but usable. The director made sure he pointed this out to me on our initial walkthrough.

"This isn't the place to be if you're trying to make a name for yourself, David," He had told me from behind his metal desk.

"This is just a hobby for most of the guys here and a good paycheck as long as you keep observing. You can look at whatever you want just so long as it's in space and you keep the log updated."

With that, he shooed me out of his office and into the waiting room of scientists. "Hobbyists" was the correct term for all of them. While they had all gone through the same college courses as I had, no one was here to prove anything. Staring at the stars was more than enough for them.

That was until I met Harry. Harry was a quiet man who kept to his desk. He hadn't shown up at the initial introduction. He had been far too busy looking at the Messier 2-star cluster. Noting little to no change, he was still convinced there had been a disturbance in that area.

Harry and I quickly became friends. We started spending our off days talking about our nights of staring into space as kids. We had shared practically the same childhood. Lying in fields and dreaming of being where we are now.

"I always wanted to go up there you know?" Harry told me after a swig of beer. "Asthma is an instant deal breaker for NASA though. Oh well - plenty of sights here to take my breath away."

"Hey, Harry," I said, rolling the beer bottle in my palms. "Did you ever shine a flashlight out of the grass at night?"

"All those creepy little eyes staring back at you?" He gave a small shiver and took another sip of his beer. "Those were the worst. Started laying on the bed of my truck after I did that once." He said shivering and drank his beer.

"What if stars were the same?" I asked him, depositing my empty bottle in the recycling bin.

"I'd say you need to lay off the horror movies my friend." He laughed "And maybe cut back on the beers."

"Yeah," I chuckled "Just a crazy thought I had a long time ago."

The weeks and months flew by as we continued observing and logging all the nebulas and galaxies we could see. Harry and I continued our friendship and did everything we could to further our careers. Sadly, with the limited technology we had at our disposal observing was the best we could do.

One late night, after far too much coffee, I noticed something odd happening in the Messier 5 cluster. It was the star cluster I had been observing for months and for a second, I couldn't locate it. I made a log of it, convinced the director would just shrug it off as operator error.

I continued observing the cluster for the next few weeks and noted anytime I couldn't locate it. After the fifteenth disappearance, I went to Harry.

"Hey, Harry?" I whispered, tapping him on the shoulder causing him to jump.

"Jesus, David!" He yelped. "Going to give someone a heart attack."

He looked visibly shaken but calmed himself quickly.

"Have you been noticing anything off lately?" I asked as I took a seat from a nearby desk.

"Look, David," Harry's voice lowered. "I don't know…we should get back to work before the director comes by." Harry turned back to his computer typing in a new log.

"You know the director isn't…" I started.

"David!" Harry whispered harshly. "Go back to your desk and get back to work."

Without another word, I got up and went back to my area. For all the time I'd known Harry, I'd never seen him angry. I sat and continued watching the cluster appear and disappear in intervals. Once the day was done and my car was warming up, Harry came up to my car.

I rolled my window down to talk to him, but before I could even begin to speak, a piece of paper was thrown in the open window and Harry was gone. I unfolded the note and read it.

"Don't say a word. Turn off your phone and meet me at the park. You know which one."

I didn't know what Harry had up his ass, but I was damn sure going to find out. A few minutes later I was parked outside Hide Park. I was scanning the empty area for Harry when a sudden knocking on the window made me jump.

A tall man in a business suit was smiling at me through the window. I rolled it down just enough so that we could have a conversation.

"I need to speak with you a moment, Doctor," The man said flashing pearly whites at me.

"I'm waiting on a friend here," I replied and began rolling up the window. "I don't need any of what you're selling."

A beep came from outside my door and I saw my door lock pop up. I was on my feet before I could even register what was happening.

"I just need a moment of your time," The man in the suit said again still flashing those teeth at me.

Two other men in suits dragged me across the lot and into a van I hadn't seen before. They threw me unceremoniously into the back and slammed the door behind me. Harry later curled up in the corner, blood trickling through what could only be a broken nose.

"Harry!" I whispered, "Harry what the fuck is going on?"

Harry's one good eye looked at me.

"Did you do what I told you to?" He mumbled through a swollen jaw. I hadn't bought into Harry's secret agent note so I'd left my phone on to listen to music. Harry saw the look on my face and laid his head down on the floor of the van.

"You stupid fucker!" Harry spat blood at me. "You've killed us both!"

"For what!" I shot back. "Noticing that our equipment is shitty and sometimes we lose entire clusters?"

"You remember our talk a while back?" Harry whispered hoarsely. "About the flashlight?"

"Yeah, what about it?" I asked.

"I laughed at you so you would put that kind of thinking behind you. I don't know if the director was drunk or high when he did your orientation or if he thought we would handle it." Harry coughed up blood and spat it to the side. "We aren't supposed to notice it. We aren't supposed to log it. And we damn sure aren't supposed to talk about it!"

"Harry, I don't understand what you're talking about," I said as I attempted to steady myself from the shaking of the van. "How the hell does this have anything to do with looking at insects in the grass?" I was thrown back as the van took off.

"Would you have known they were there if you hadn't shone your light?" Harry asked.

"Well, no I knew they were there, but I couldn't see them," I said.

"The insects didn't know you were there either until you shone your light on them." Harry sat up unsteadily. "We look at them, and they know it. But we aren't supposed to know that they are looking back."

The van came to a lurching halt. Two sets of doors slammed simultaneously and the crunch of boots made their way to the back of the van. I braced myself, waiting for the doors to swing open. Instead, the van began to inch forward. I looked over to Harry confusion plastered across my face.

Harry stared back at me. I could see his mind turning, attempting to figure out what was going on. I saw the realization hit him and then gravity let go. Lights swirled around the rear windows as my stomach settled back into position. A shadow passed along the window followed by a massive eye.

The Director

"That movie was awesome! Those critics have no clue what they are talking about." I yelled to no one except the fly trying to force its way out of the forcefield that was my grimy window. I'm a self-proclaimed movie snob. My days consist of reading online reviews of bad movies, proving them wrong, and then arguing online for hours. Since my days are filled with such excitement my time for company is very limited hence the empty room into which I was yelling. One scathing comment thread later the critic's poor tastes I decided my bed was calling for me.

I always wished days went by like they did in movies. Skip all the unnecessaries, and do a montage to pass the mundane by, but no I'm stuck going through the motions with not even a laugh track or applause sign. I blame my dad for my warped mind. At the age of eight he bought me a VCR and TV combo along with an assortment of VHS tapes. Dad never really tried to curb my soon-to-be addiction. If anything, he tried to feed into it. Providing me with new movies regularly.

Film school was my calling after high school. Dad paid a good bit of the tuition and for my dingey little basement apartment with his life insurance policy. The rest came from the meager check I got from best buy selling old folks' stuff they will never fully use. I saved and scrimped; lived off ramen and coupons to buy myself a decent cinecamera. My plan was simply to direct B-movies and work my way up to being a world-class director. Finals came and my wealthy future dream was put on hold for a bit.

I passed the midterms now on to a wonderful and well-needed break from all things school related. Even though I say a break is needed, my passion for movies kind of contradicts that. I decided to spend my time at the local coffee shop enjoying the atmosphere and great coffee while engrossed in the latest horror movies.

A sudden prod in the shoulder brought me back to my senses with a startled jump. It was a young man with unruly hair. I know I've seen him before, but I couldn't figure out where.

"Hey, is that return of the body worm?"

"Um, yeah, it is. Do I know you?"

"Oh sorry, I guess I should start with my name. I'm Luke and I go to the same school. I've seen you around campus." Luke extended his hand out to me.

"I'm Nate. I knew you looked familiar. Do you like these kinds of movies?" I asked taking the offered hand.

Luke and I spent the rest of the break almost inseparable. We would spend most nights at my place watching a movie and then posting arguments online continuing the conversations for hours. Reality eventually caught up to us and we were forced to resume our school obligations. Luke and I kept in touch, but I felt like the bond we had shared just wasn't the same without our shared interest. Until he came to me with a proposition just before the summer break.

I was in film school for an actual career Luke on the other hand was in it to make a name for himself. Sure, Luke had the looks, but his acting was stiff and not natural at all. The only time he came to life was watching horror shows. Luke met me for lunch the day before the end of the semester and asked if I would help him with his assignment.

"Look my professor is a hard ass, Nate. I need a little help from you and your camera."

"What exactly is it you need me to do?" I asked putting down my coffee.

"We kind of have to write and film a thirty-minute horror film."

"I'm game man, but what kind of professor would make you do that on your break?"

"I told you dude he's a hard ass."

A week later we were huddled up in my apartment putting together a hasty script for the movie. It was not going to be a masterpiece by any means but passing was the goal. It took a week to finish, mostly because we took quite a few movie breaks. The main problem had not even been confronted yet, who was going to act in our movie? Luke couldn't act in multiple parts no matter how good or bad his acting was.

After a few days of asking around and getting nowhere, Luke found a homeless couple whose only stipulation was a few warm meals and twenty bucks each. Luke didn't mind ponying up for it. We all loaded it into my van and made our way north to Luke's family farm. Our movie had a haunted cornfield and a cornfield on an abandoned farm was the perfect venue.

While I got my camera set up Luke briefed our actors on how the movie would progress and went over the script with them. They were fairly quick on the uptake so all in all a pretty painless experience. We did a few dry runs to make sure we all knew our places and when to be where. Once we had a good understanding of everything, we went out for a bite to eat.

Our actors were nice enough people. They had been traveling across the country and were taking a break when we approached them. After our bellies were full, we decided it was time to get started. The night was here, and the moon was in the perfect phase for a nighttime shot. Once we got back to the cornfield we immediately got started.

"Oh no Jim I hear something coming from the cornfield." Sara our female actress whispered.

"Don't worry Sara. There's nothing here that can hurt us." Jim responded.

"But Jim can't you hear that?"

"It's just the wind Sara."

B-rated movie at its finest, but like I said passing was fine. I can direct an actual blockbuster later. The actors continued with the script, and I saw Luke getting into position wearing his ridiculous easter bunny mask. For whatever reason, he had to have a mask and all the others would have broken some copyright infringement law out there.

"Jim seriously, I'm getting the creeps let's just go!"

"Fine Sara, I guess you won't get the surprise I had for you."

"Jim, Who's that?"

"What are you talking about there's no one..."

I panned out to Luke standing menacingly in a small clearing. It was at this point he was supposed to start his slow march toward the actors. Luke stood fixed in place. I couldn't tell what was going through his mind, but he wasn't following the script. Jim took a step towards Luke and prompted him.

"Look man we're sorry for trespassing. We're leaving, okay?" That unscripted line seemed to shock Luke into action.

He took a few lumbering steps toward the two. Jim backpedaled as Sara held his arm. Once they got their bearings back, they took off. I followed in right behind them fighting my way through the corn stalks. Luke followed the script loosely, which was fine by me. A director has to be up for some creative liberties.

Jim got tangled up by a couple of bunched-up stalks. Sara kept going a few steps just by sheer momentum and Luke descended on Jim instantly. Let me say Jim was a damn good actor for twenty bucks. His screams were so real and the blood packs we made worked like a charm. Sara even got really into it; her face was a mask of pure horror.

Luke finally stopped his stabbing spree and rose from Jim to face Sara. My adrenaline was running wild. Screw passing Luke was getting an A+. Sara took off and I followed behind as fast as I could, but she was outdoing herself. Luke was coming in hot, and it took everything my legs could muster to stay within shooting distance.

Luke descended on her and knocked her flat pretty hard. I was worried she might have gotten hurt from the fall. She turned to him immediately and began fighting him off. I have got to say we landed some really good actors for dirt cheap.

"Get off of me!" Sara yelled at Luke. In between punches, she turned to me. "He's dead! Why are you still filming?"

Great, now I got to edit that out later. Luke wasted no time in "ending" her. He continued stabbing her over, and over again. Her screams were so realistic. Once she finally stopped, Luke rose and stared into the camera. He was supposed to slowly walk towards the camera, but I was a fan of the stare-down even more. I stopped recording and approached Luke and Sara.

"Sara come on let's go. That was awesome! Jim's probably waiting for us."

Sara wasn't moving so I went over to her to help her up. Her eyes were glossy, I knelt thinking maybe Luke scared her a little too much and put her in a state of shock. When I realized she wasn't breathing I panicked.

"Luke what did you..."

He was gone, I felt for Sara's pulse and found nothing. I trudged through the field listening carefully for footsteps. I found Jim in the same place we had left him. I checked for a pulse and emptied what was left of my dinner on the ground next to him. I had just watched Luke murder two people.

"I can leave. just get in the van, burn the tape, and go far away."

I repeated to myself until I realized I had just left my DNA all over the crime scene! Then it hit me, Luke was still here somewhere. I hadn't heard the van startup; he could be hiding anywhere. I made my way back to the lot to the van. To my surprise, it was perfectly fine, tires intact and keys still in the ignition not your typical horror movie moment. I went in and checked the back. I wasn't going to let the stereotypes be my downfall. I started the van and got the hell out of there. I made my way back to my apartment contemplating whether to call the police or just go on the run. I opened my door cautiously checking every nook, cranny, and door for Luke. I even checked under the bed just to be sure. There was a bloodstained note with a bloody knife stabbed into the back of my front door.

"That was fun Nate. Thanks for the help."

I called the police and was placed in custody immediately. The judge found me guilty of assisted homicide and gave me ten years. I spent five years in a minimum-security prison and got an early release for good conduct. I moved to a run-down apartment and found a crap maintenance job that would hire an ex-con.

I was moving on pretty well with my life. I still had dreams of that night, but with therapy and medication, I could sleep most nights. They never found Luke and the video was lost during a transfer. My anxiety was always high when I came home or got in my car. I kept expecting Luke at every turn. I would get scared every time I turned on the TV expecting the video to be playing.

I got a package in the mail today with no return address. I opened the box to find a VHS tape surrounded by bubble wrap. I popped it into the VHS player already knowing what it would show. I recognized Jim and Sara instantly. I sat through the movie I had filmed cursing myself for not realizing something so obvious. I really thought they were acting. When the movie came to Luke just standing there a caption popped up.

"Keep going."

I sat through another movie of the same design. The camera angles were horrible, and the cast was lacking, but I sat through it anyway. In the end, the camera dropped, and you saw Luke walking forward. Offscreen, you hear a blood-curdling scream. A few moments later Luke comes back into focus.

"You were a great director Nate. This guy didn't even come close. I'd love to hear your critiques on this one."

Luke picked the camera up.

"Oh, and I can't wait to share the rest of my work with you Nate. You're a good director but an even better critic."

Tap

Tap

Tap

Tap

"Look, John," Sara said. "If you're that bored you don't have to watch the movie."

"I'm fine," I replied. "I promise just little muscle twitches you know."

The movie had started only 30 minutes ago. I had suggested it to keep her occupied for some time so I could deal with my thoughts. I really needed to make a call, but I didn't want to move. I didn't want Sara to get concerned.

Tap

Tap

Tap

"Do you want to go take a breather outside?" Sara suggested.

"I'm telling you, I'm fine," I snapped. "Just trust me, please."

"Okay, then, grumpy." Sara huffed and focused herself on the tv again.

My phone sat in the kitchen, and my concentration was stretched to the max. I had to figure out a way to get us out of this situation, and her constant questioning wasn't helping. I had to think, I had to figure it out quickly.

Tap

Tap

"Seriously, John, what the -" Sara started again.

Tap

"John!" Sara lost it. "Stop it now! You're ruining the movie!"

"Sara, sweetheart," I pleaded. "Please - for me - just let me do this okay?"

"Why?" Sara asked.

Tap

Tap

Tap

"You know what," Sara got up. "Don't even bother. I'm going to bed!"

With that she stormed off.

I didn't even move my head. The last time I looked away from the window, it had moved about 50 yards. I could only make out the silhouette before that. Once I looked away and looked back, it had been standing not even ten feet from the window. It moved in between blinks until I could make out its pitch-black eyes after just a few minutes.

Its smile stretched as its gaze had met mine then he had lifted a bony finger. Sara had mistaken the taps for my boredom, but luckily with her gone, I could focus on this thing without her noticing. A loud ring startled me, and I glanced at the kitchen where my phone was dancing along the countertop, I tore my gaze away and back to the window.

A frost-etched smiley face was crudely drawn in the pane where the black-eyed man had stood seconds ago.

Tap

Tap

Tap

"John," Sara yelled from the bedroom. "Enough with the damn tapping! Hurry up and come to bed."

"Just a moment," I responded.

"And close the window, please," She added. "All the heat is getting out, and I'm not getting back up."

Blink

(This is a continuation of the story "tap")

"John, we need you to tell us what happened to Sara." The detective said again.

"I've already told you everything!" I exclaimed. "How many more times do you want me to repeat the same story?"

I sighed as I stared down at the now cold cup of coffee.

blink

"John, I know this is tough on you," The detective shuffled crime scene photographs around on the table. "We need to make sure you didn't miss any details. as it stands now, we have you booked on first-degree murder."

I stared at the photos for a long moment. My Sara lay sprawled in unnatural poses in the photos. Blood covered every surface in the photos. Her face distorted in a stiff silent scream.

blink

"I came upstairs and saw her bleeding out everywhere," I said, my voice barely a whisper. I was beginning to grow numb to the memories. "I ran to her and got her blood all over me from holding her. Then I pulled the knife from her stomach to try and put pressure on the wound. No, we didn't fight. No, we weren't cheating on each other, and no, I didn't pull out a life insurance policy days before this happened."

I took a sip of the coffee grimacing at the taste and rested my head on the cool metal of the desk.

blink

"Oh, but you did fight." A soft whisper echoed through the room. The voice startled me causing me to bump into the table sending pictures to the floor.

I looked up at the detective only to find myself staring back into two milky white eyes. A commercial white smile spread upon the face of the creature I had encountered the night before. Its skin was rotten and black causing the teeth and eyes to stand out in contrast.

"Hello, John," The creature whispered.

blink

I knew once I'd done it the creature would move. It would be right in front of my face or behind me. To my surprise, once I opened my eyes again the creature was still seated across from me. It smiled patiently.

"Why didn't you tell them about me?" The creature whispered again. Its rotten hands spread the pictures on the table for a better view.

"If I told them a creature that could move faster than a blink broke into my house and killed Sara I'd be locked in an insane asylum by now." My voice cracked as I spoke.

"I'm going to make a deal with you, John," The creature's face lit up as it settled on a picture on the table. Its hands scooped it up and stashed it in the interior of the hoodie it wore. "You intrigue me."

blink

The creature now stood next to me. Startled, I recoiled away from it, making me lose balance and knock over my chair. It was on me in a flash, face mere inches from my own. I could smell the rot coming from its blackened skin.

"You are the first person in eons to look me in the face and not run screaming," He hissed out melodically. "The hunt has gotten boring because as soon as their little back is turned, there I am." He punctuated the last part of his sentence with taps to my nose. The thin finger leaving flakes of dead skin on my face.

blink

I found myself upright again and staring into those milky eyes from across the table. The cuffs that had been keeping me in the chair no longer pressed into me. I looked at the table to see the pictures had been swept away into their folder and my coffee cup was now steaming.

"Ready to hear my deal, John?" The creature steepled its fingers in a business-like pose.

"Do I have a choice?" I asked rubbing my wrist. The creature feigned a shocked face placing a hand on its chest.

"You have a choice, John. You always have a choice." The smile on the creature's face turned predatory. The comically white teeth had turned pointed and yellowed. "You can choose not to listen, and I can choose to be hungry."

A deep laugh filled the room as the creature threw its head back. I took the opportunity that was given and flung the steaming coffee at that rotting face. A shriek filled the room as steam rose from between its fingers. I urged my muscles into action and pushed the table over coming down on top of it and the now burnt creature.

blink

"You're pissing me off, John," The creature's voice had doubled, taking on a plaintive and demanding quality at the same time. "Fine, no deal for you. Instead, you're going to be my new toy until I've had my fill!" I lay on top of the overturned table searching for the voice.

"I'm going to wipe every bit of this from your memory," He explained. "When you come to, you won't remember Sara or me. You'll go back to your mundane life, and I'll go back to hunting. Then once you've moved on and found yourself your one love again. Well, there I'll be and this time I'm going to take my time." The lights went out in the interrogation room. A single light flicked on behind the glass pane in the wall illuminating the creatures' black figure and white smile.

blink

"I'll be that little shadow in the corner of your eye." The creature's voice now whispered close enough that I could feel its breath on my skin.

blink

"I'll be the shadowy figure in the corner of the room." White teeth appeared inches from my face. A charred tongue licked hungrily at nonexistent lips.

blink

"And once I've got you so scared that sleep becomes nothing but a passing dream, that's when I'll take everything from you, John." Hands gripped my shoulders and lifted me to my feet. " And I won't stop there. Once I've taken everything from you, I'll offer you my deal again. If you piss me off, then we repeat this little song and dance all over again."

blink

"Goodbye John."

The sound of birds chirping pulled me from a fitful dream. I got up and stretched my arms and legs feeling as though I'd run a marathon in my sleep. I noticed a shadow at the corner of my eye and began to rub the sleep from them as I proceeded to the bathroom.

blink

If you made it this far with your sanity, then I congratulate you.

Thank you for reading these haunting tales made by an independent author.

If you are a return reader, then thank you for sticking with me.

If you are a new reader, then thank you for giving me a shot.

Independent authors live by reviews and word of mouth. If you enjoyed the stories, feel free to leave some kind words wherever you purchased this product. If that doesn't suit you feel free to reach out to me on social media. My tik tok account is the easiest way to find me.

9 7 9 8 8 6 9 2 4 4 1 8 5